NoNieqa Ramos

Illustrated by
Jacqueline Alcántara

Versify
HOUGHTON MIFFLIN HARCOURT
Boston New York

all frosting, powdered sugar, and pastries.

Leaves love notes in your almuerzo, homemade.
She's the cinnamon to your tembleque,
the tres leches to your cake.

she like a marine.
Up three flights of stairs, carries
the groceries.

When you *both* had that fever,
carried you to emergency.

she could have her own clothing line.

The way she walks into a room–
SHUU!–
she's an ad for
fancy perfume.

Nobody could
walk in her
high-heel shoes.

That’s why you couldn’t help
messing with the makeup
she keeps in her purse.
You want to look just like her.
But—

YOUR MAMA SO FORGIVING,
SHE LETS YOU KEEP ON LIVING.
WEPA!

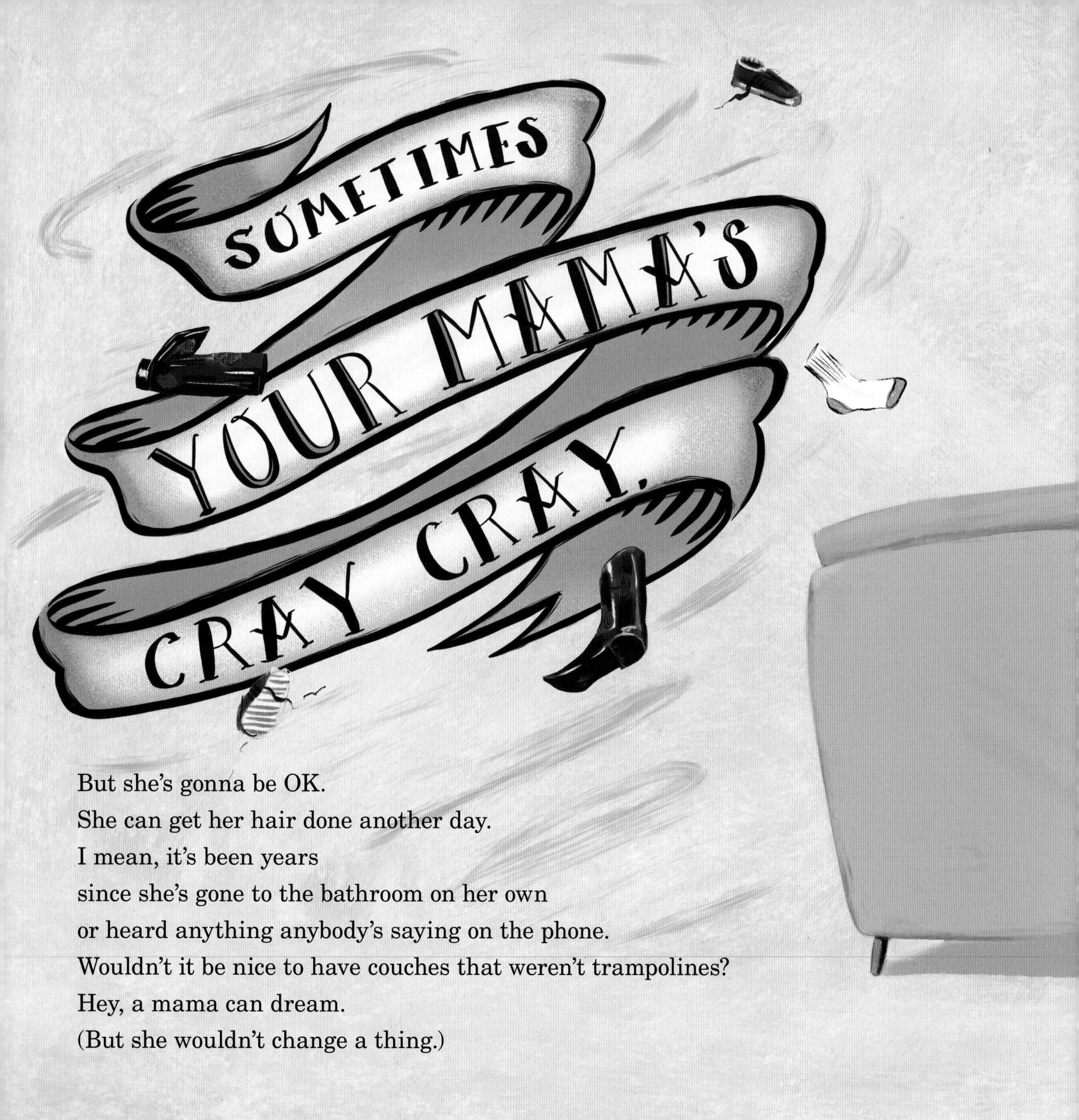

But she's gonna be OK.
She can get her hair done another day.
I mean, it's been years
since she's gone to the bathroom on her own
or heard anything anybody's saying on the phone.
Wouldn't it be nice to have couches that weren't trampolines?
Hey, a mama can dream.
(But she wouldn't change a thing.)

YOUR MAMA A BRAINIAC—

mo' betta than any app.
A drone? She'll teach you to
work it from her phone.

Got math problems?
She could solve 'em.

Plus, you're both library VIPs,
'cause she knows errything 'bout errything.
She's your A-Team.

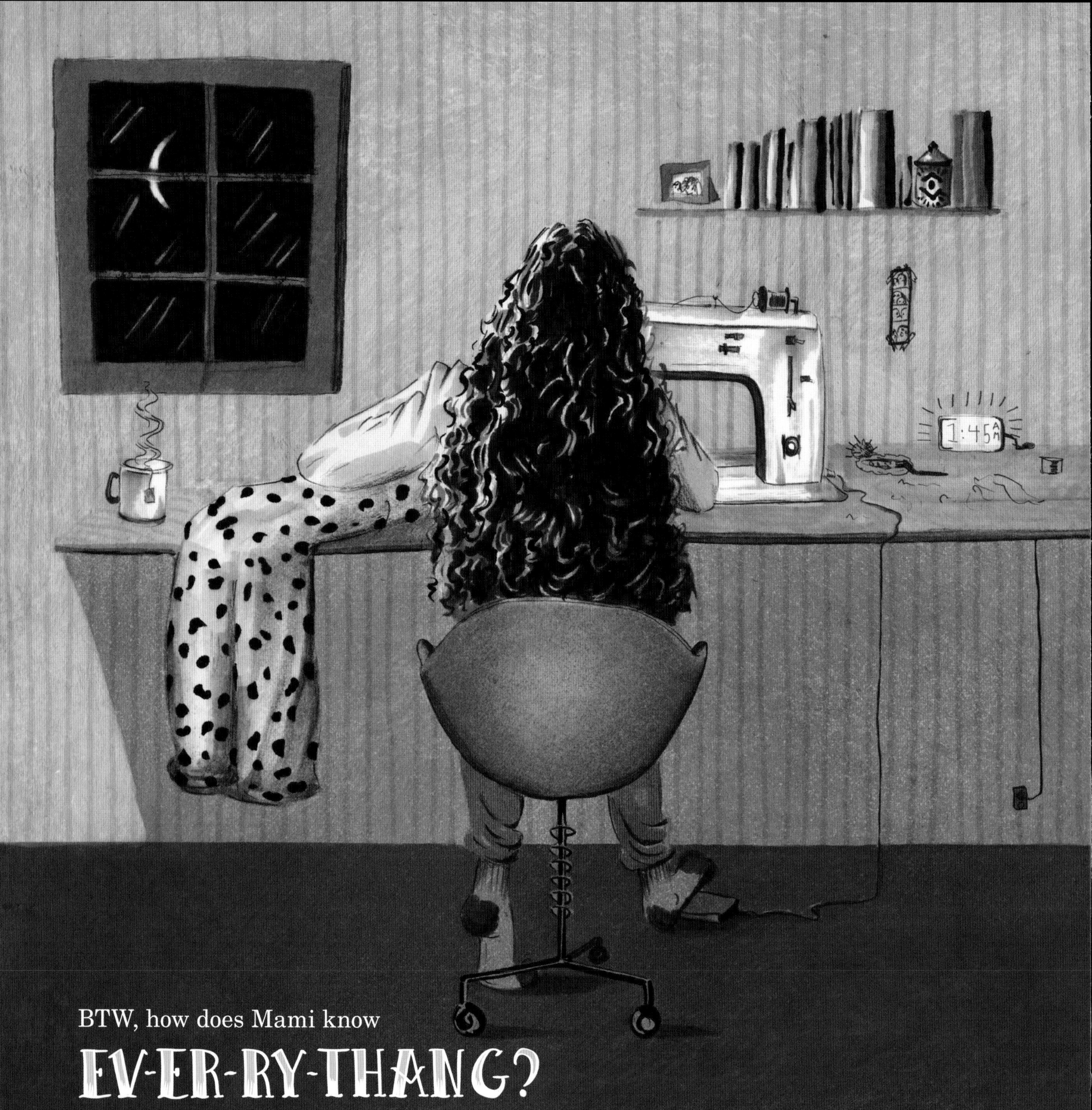

BTW, how does Mami know

EV-ER-RY-THANG?

Woman catches all your vibes;
must read minds.

That's how she slays
birthdays, holidays, anniversaries,
weekends, vacays, getaways.

You can hardly wait.
She's got road trips whipped,
and that's not even the half of it.

YOUR MAMA

SO FUNNY,

the dinner table is her stage.
She starts up with "Back in the day–"
and you can hardly wait.

She keeps the jokes cookin',
the comida deliciosa and warm.
She got everybody beggin' for more.

she gonna stand by and watch injustice?

Nope.
She takes all you kids
when she votes.
With posters homemade,
she marches in every parade.

She got friends
at work, at church,
around the 'hood.
Life is good.

She got cousins by the dozens,
hermanos in droves,
and you, her gold.

She loves you more
than you'll ever know.

You're her
WISH,
her
HOPE,
her
PRAYER,
her
PUSH,
her
PULL,
her
MIRACLE.

YOUR MAMA'S ALL THAT.
SO LET'S GIVE HER
TWO SNAPS, A CIRCLE,
AND A

MAD DAP,
A HUG,
AND
A KISS.
TWIST.

Let's raise the roof–
woot woot–
because it takes two:

#TRUTH
#TRUTH

hmhbooks.com

The illustrations in this book were created using markers, pastels, Procreate, and Adobe Photoshop.
The text was set in New Century Schoolbook.
Cover design by Andrea Miller
Interior design by Whitney Leader-Picone and Andrea Miller

Library of Congress Cataloging-in-Publication Data
Names: Ramos, NoNieqa, author. | Alcántara, Jacqueline, illustrator.
Title: Your mama / NoNieqa Ramos, Jacqueline Alcántara.
Description: Boston : Houghton Mifflin Harcourt, 2021. | Audience: Ages 4 to 7 | Audience: Grades K–1 | Summary: Illustrations and easy-to-read text twist classic "your mama" jokes into a celebration of the beauty, power, and love of motherhood.
Identifiers: LCCN 2019047523 | ISBN 9781328631886 (hardcover)
Subjects: CYAC: Mothers—Fiction.
Classification: LCC PZ7.1.R3656 You 2021 | DDC [E]—dc23
LC record available at https://lccn.loc.gov/2019047523

Manufactured in China
SCP 10 9 8 7 6 5 4 3 2 1
4500816112